The Magic Sewing Machine

SUNNY WARNER

HOUGHTON MIFFLIN COMPANY BOSTON
1997

Walter Lorraine  Books

For information about this and other Houghton Mifflin trade
and reference books and multimedia products, visit the Bookstore
at Houghton Mifflin on the World Wide Web at
http://www.hmco.com/trade/.

Library of Congress Cataloging-in-Publication Data
Warner, Sunny.
    The magic sewing machine / Sunny Warner.
        P.   cm.
    Summary: An orphaned brother and sister are saved from the cruelty
of the orphange's headmistress by a magic sewing machine and the
goodness of their hearts.
    ISBN 0-395-82747-7
    [1. Brothers and sisters—Fiction. 2. Orphans—Fiction.
3. Orphanges—Fiction. 4. Sewing machines—Fiction.] I. Title.
PZ7.W24646Mag 1997
[E]—dc20

96-A4221
CIP
AC

Printed in the United States of America.
HOR 10 9 8 7 6 5 4 3 2 1

This book is for my daughter Jennifer,
and for Mary, Annie, Donna, Ramsey, Phyllis, and Jackie,
and for my sons Michael and Geoffrey,
with love and gratitude to each and all.

Once, in a small house, in a small village, a young girl named Olya and her little brother, Sacha, lived with their cat, Basil. They were alone in the world. To pay the rent, Olya sewed shirts for the landlord and Sacha gathered wood.

They had sold almost everything they had, except their mother's sewing machine. She had told them, "You must always keep the sewing machine. It will help you when all else fails."

The landlord told Olya she had to sew more shirts because he was raising the rent. "If you don't get them done, I will take the sewing machine, and you and your brother will be off to the orphanage." Olya sewed and sewed, but she could never sew enough.

At night, when Olya tucked Sacha into bed, they would talk about running away to find a circus. "I could sew beautiful clothes for the acrobats," Olya would say. And then, half asleep, Sacha would say, "And I could train the lions and tigers."

One morning, a tall figure came to their door and said:
"I'm Miss Schnaap from the orphanage. I've come to get you."
She stepped inside and looked around.
"Well you don't have much. Can you run that sewing machine?"
"Yes I can. I made shirts for the rent," answered Olya.
"Good. You can sew for me at the orphanage," said Miss Schnaap.

As they were leaving, the landlord stopped them.
"That sewing machine is mine! It's owed me for rent!"
"FIDDLESTICKS! This sewing machine is coming with me to the orphanage," thundered Miss Schnaap, and she gave him such a steely glare that the landlord turned pale and let them pass.

Miss Schnaap ordered Olya and Sacha and Basil into her wagon and took them to the orphanage.

At the orphanage it was dark and cold. Miss Schnaap told them, "You will see to it that your work is done. Lazy children do not eat. Naughty children and children who cry are put in this closet. It gives them time to think."

Sacha went to work with the other children making baskets. Olya worked in the attic where she sewed clothes for Miss Schnaap. Basil was put in the cellar to catch mice.

The children did the cleaning, the mending, the laundry, and the ironing. They made repairs, chopped wood, and scrubbed floors. They did their best, but almost every night there was a child in the closet whose work had failed to satisfy Miss Schnaap.

They did the cooking and served Miss Schnaap her meals. She liked sausage for breakfast. They had gruel. She liked roast chicken for lunch. They had turnips. She liked a nice bit of beef for supper. They had the drippings on their bread.

Every Friday Miss Schnaap went to town to sell the baskets the children had made. She bought food for the children, but she never bought enough, because she was filling her mattress with most of the money. The lumpier it got, the better she slept.

Late one icy night the children were visiting Olya up in the attic. She was trying to finish the day's sewing, though her hands were numb with cold.

Painted on the sewing machine in tiny golden script were words Olya had read many times before.

> *If your heart be true, and your purpose love,*
> *Then I will stitch your every wish.*

Tonight the words seemed to dance strangely in the candlelight as she sewed. She glanced up at the children gathered around her. She could see that Masha's bare feet were blue with cold.

Olya said, *"I wish* Masha had some warm *boots!"* There was a sudden sharp whirr, and two fat little boots flew across the room.

"Olya! It's because you wished! Wish again!" said Sacha. "A warm dress," said Olya, working the pedal, "Warm stockings!" and out of the humming machine flew a dress and stockings, just Masha's size.

And then there were warm clothes for Nadia! for Boris! for Sacha! Warm clothes and featherbeds and quilts flew through the air for Alexi, for Maria, until each child, warm and happy, was dancing to the song of the sewing machine. Suddenly, Sacha said, "SHHH! we will wake Miss Schnaap!"

At once, everyone was very quiet.
Sacha said, "We must find a way out of this terrible place."
Maybe the sewing machine can help!" said Olya.
"How? Can it sew us each a pair of wings?" said Alexi.
"Or—maybe some flying carpets?" said Nadia.

"Wait!" said Sacha.

"We could fly away on some balloons!
Some of those great big ones." Olya pedaled the sewing machine.
"Make us a balloon," said Sacha. "A balloon, a balloon, we need a big balloon,"
said Alexi and Boris, Nadia and Masha, but very quietly.
There was a sharp whirr, and then something almost
as big as the attic began rising out of the sewing machine.
It rose until it bumped against the rafters,
and then it stopped.
"Hurray!" said Sacha, "A balloon!"
"It's beautiful," whispered Olya.
"I'll get one of the big baskets and
we can tie it on,"
said Nadia.

"But," said Boris, "we have to cut a hole in the roof."
And that's what they did, as quietly as they could.

Little Masha went down to the kitchen
with Olya to pack some supplies, very quietly.

When everything was ready, Sacha said,
"Who wants to be first?"
"ME!" said Alexi, and he was about to climb
into the basket, when suddenly

the terrible roar of Miss Schnaap was heard. "WHAT IS THE MEANING OF THIS?"

After casting a glance at the enormous balloon, Miss Schnaap stuck her head into the basket to see what might be inside.

It was at that moment that the balloon broke through the roof,
lifting off so suddenly that Miss Schnaap tipped over into the basket.

By the time she was right side up again, she was too far away for anyone to hear her.

"Goodbye, Miss Schnaap," called the children, waving at the balloon. They waved until it disappeared completely.

After they were sure it was truly gone, the children hugged each other good night and climbed into bed. That night they dreamed they drifted past icy stars and falling snow, while deep in their warm new featherbeds.

The next day, Olya and Masha found the money in Miss Schnaap's mattress. "We're rich!" Olya sang. "We can buy all the food in the world! Sausages! Bread! Butter! Herring! Pretty little potatoes!" She and Masha jumped into the wagon and sang all the way to town.

And that day they made an enormous feast.

The mayor came by and was surprised to find that Miss Schnaap had gone. When he saw that everything was in order, he left Olya in charge until her return. The children raised a great cheer. Somehow they did not think Miss Schnaap would be returning any time soon.

That was the coldest winter in memory, but the children were all snug in the orphanage. They had made it warm and bright with hangings and curtains Olya made on the sewing machine and with merry fires in every stove.

People from the village loved to visit. They taught the children the things they knew: how to read, write, and do numbers; how to juggle and walk a tightrope; how to play the violin and the piccolo.

And that was how the orphanage became the Academy of Circus Arts.

Olya, Sacha, and Basil celebrated their good fortune every day. At night, the sight of the starry sky always made the children remember the wonderful balloon. They would smile and say, "GOOD NIGHT, MISS SCHNAAP, WHEREVER YOU ARE!"